Marsh Jordan

Latest Styles

Fall and Winter 93-94

Marsh Jordan

Latest Styles
Fall and Winter 93-94

ISBN/EAN: 9783337255831

Printed in Europe, USA, Canada, Australia, Japan

Cover: Foto ©Andreas Hilbeck / pixelio.de

More available books at **www.hansebooks.com**

Announcement.

NORTH.

WEST. EAST.

SOUTH.

ANOTHER season rolls around, and once again we send our greetings to thousands of patrons scattered all over the habitable globe. The benefits of distant shopping by mail are now universally appreciated, and the name of JORDAN, MARSH & CO. is known wherever postage stamps are used.

As in the past so shall we in the future endeavor to merit patronage. The season of 1893-94 finds us better equipped than ever to attend to our customers' wishes. The fashion centres of Europe have yielded their choicest conceptions, and America's best offerings are carried in our stock. In prices we are unquestionably the lowest; and our name is a sufficient guarantee as to reliability.

Respectfully yours,

JORDAN, MARSH & CO.,

BOSTON, MASS.

BOSTON, MASS.

6011. 6007.

No. 6011. English Cashmere Suit, trimmed with braid. All colors. New wide skirt. Price, $8.75.

No. 6007. All-wool fancy hop sacking, in all the popular shades, trimmed with serpentine mohair braid on waist and skirt. Price, $16.75.

BOSTON, MASS.

6015.   6016.

No. 6015. All-wool cashmere, trimmed with imported crochet and satin gimps. In black and brown.   Price, $18.00.

No. 6016. Fine all-wool serge, trimmed on waist and skirt with fine fancy mohair braid. Skirt 4½ yards wide. Can be had in black and blue.   Price, $25.00.

BOSTON, MASS.

8005.   8009.

No. 8005. Gray mixture Suit, made with double-breasted waist and large buttons on waist. Price, $7.50.

No. 8009. Suit, can be had in 20 different shades, such as gray, brown, blue, etc. Price, $8.50.

BOSTON, MASS.

446.   504.

No. 446. Made of chintz, with butterfly ruffle, full puff sleeves with deep cuff, Watteau back, loose front. In dark colors with flower combinations. Price, $1.35.

No. 504. Made of striped Saxony flannel, with ruffle over shoulder extending to the waist, trimmed with velvet ribbon, Watteau back and loose front shirred at the neck, and tight-fitting inside waist. All colors. Price, $3.50.

BOSTON, MASS.

510. 506.

No. 510. Made of cashmere delaine, with ruffle over shoulder meeting belt at the waist, trimmed with rick-rack braid, full empire sleeve and deep cuff. Dark colors with flower patterns. Price, $2.00.

No. 506. Made of teazle down, with shoulder cape split in back, full sleeve with deep cuff, cape collar, belt, and sleeves trimmed with rick-rack braid. In all colors. Price, $2.25.

861.   879.

No. 861.   Made with tucked yoke, Watteau back, and cape on shoulders.   In choice styles and standard prints.   Price, $1.50.

No. 879.   Gallateer cloth.   Styles selected especially for the garments.   Made with shirred front, Watteau back, and three capes on shoulders.   Price, $3.25.

2577.   6246.

No. 2577.   Fine cashmere Tea-Gown, trimmed with two double capes of embroidery to form a zouave front; draped sleeves with fancy cuff of embroidery.   Price, $6.75.

No. 6246.   Eiderdown, sailor collar and cuffs, with ruffled ribbon.   Price, $7.50.

BOSTON, MASS.

6215.   6252.

No. 6215. Henrietta, with Jabot lace front and back, velvet ribbon around armholes, full sleeve with double ruffle, edged on velvet on cap of sleeve, Medici collar, lace and velvet. Price, $10.00.

No. 6252. Pinked flannel, with yoke of plaid goods, feather-stitched rolling collar, and coat sleeve with pinked cuff. Price, $10.50.

BOSTON, MASS.

229.

342.

236.

No. 229. Cheviot Coat, new umbrella collar trimmed with imitation mink, 32 inches long, half lined. Price, $15.00.

No. 342. Kersey Jacket, 34 inches long, collar lined with silk, new back and sleeves, half lined and tight fitting. Comes in all the leading shades. Price, $12.75.

No. 236. Beaver Jacket, 32 inches long. New cape collar edged with electric seal, new style back. Price, $10.50.

170.   731.   320.

No. 170.   Cheviot-finish Cloth Jacket, with large umbrella collar, 30 inches long.   Colors, black, blue, and brown.   Price, $5.00.
No. 731.   Reefer Jacket, Melton cheviot, half lined, new style sleeves.   Colors, blue, black, and Havana.   Price, $5.00.
No. 764.   Same style as above.   Cashmere cheviot, 32 inches long, half lined.   In black, blue, Havana, and tan.   Price, $7.50
and $10.00.
No. 320.   Columbia Collar Tailor-made Jacket, made of fine all-wool beaver, extra large sleeves, tight-fitting back.   Price, $15.00.

309.

153.

321.

No. 309. Tailor-made Coat, made of good quality beaver, trimmed with pulled coney. Colors, black, blue, and brown. Price, $12.00.

No. 153. Fancy Cloth Jacket of good material, cape collar trimmed with pulled coney, new back and sleeves. Price, $8.75.

No. 321. Kersey Cape Coat, 34 inches long, umbrella collar lined with silk, half lined and tight fitting, new full sleeves. Colors, black and blue. Price, $12.75.

501.   509.   510.

501.   Ladies' Wrap, made of fine imported clay diagonal, lined through with silk serge, handsomely embroidered.   Price, $16.50.

509.   Ladies' Wrap, made of fine diagonal, lined all through with quilted satin lining Price, $12.75.

510.   Ladies' Wrap, of fine clay diagonal, handsomely embroidered in silk, and lined through with black quilted satin.   Price, $13.75.

BOSTON, MASS.

One of the Popular Styles for this season is
.Seal Plush Garments.

799.   273.   1206.

No. 799. Cape made of fine plush, 30 inches long, new collar and Watteau plait, good quality lining. Price, $13.75.

No. 273. Tight-fitting Plush Coat, new style collar, trimmed with electric seal. Price, $25.00.

No. 1206. Seal Plush Cape, 28 inches long, satin lined. Price, $10.00.

BOSTON, MASS.

MACKINTOSH AND CRAVENETTE DEPARTMENT.

WE desire to call attention to our Mackintosh, Gossamer, and Cravenette Department, which has no equal in the country. As regards variety, styles, quality, and prices, we are the acknowledged leaders, receiving daily all the newest and most effective designs and fabrics.

Misses' Waterproof Circulars, . . $1.25
   "   "   Peasant, with cape, 2.00
Ladies' Plain Circulars, black and
   gray, ... 1.25, 1.50, 1.75
Ladies' Inverness, black, gray, and
   brown, ... 3.00
Ladies' Inverness, black and blue, . 5.50
Ladies' Inverness, in fancy checks, 7.50

Mackintoshes and Cravenettes,
$10.50 to $20.00.

ALLIGATOR WATERPROOF.
Price, $2.00.

This is our trade-mark for one of the greatest bargains ever offered in a Gossamer Rubber Waterproof. It is manufactured for us alone, and under our special supervision. The shape is perfectly new, has all the latest improvements, is guaranteed perfectly waterproof, and fully worth $3.00.

CRAVENETTE GARMENT.

Price, $10.00.

BOSTON, MASS.

JORDAN, MARSH AND COMPANY,

RULES FOR SELF-MEASUREMENT
FOR
COSTUMES MADE TO ORDER ONLY.

The following rules for self-measurement will be found a valuable guide to those of our customers who propose ordering by mail.

CATALOGUE COSTUMES AND GARMENTS.

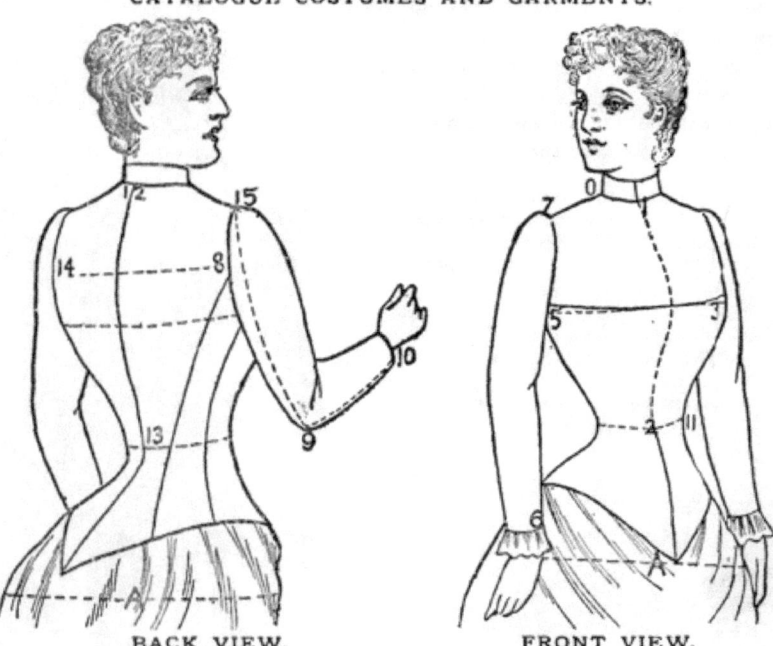

BACK VIEW.   **FRONT VIEW.**

Waist.— 12 to 13, length of back to waist.
     8 to 14, across back.
     15 to 9, shoulder to elbow.
     9 to 10, elbow to wrist.
Skirt. — Length in front from waist.
     Length in back from waist.
     Belt measure.

1, around the neck.
1 to 2, neck to waist.
3 to 5, bust, to be taken all around under arms.
5 to 6, length of sleeve inside.
0 to 7, length of shoulder.
3 to 11, from under arm to waist.
11, size of waist, all around.
A.— Around hips.

COSTUMES.
Bust measure and length of skirt in front.

CLOAKS AND JACKETS.
Bust measure only.

TEA-GOWNS.
Bust measure and length in front from neck to bottom of skirt.

We keep on hand a large assortment of all Catalogue Suits and Garments in every size, from 32-inch to 46-inch bust. Should extra large sizes be required, we should have to charge a trifle more pro rata. It occasionally happens that special sizes have to be made. In such cases a week's delay is unavoidable.

BOSTON, MASS.

No. 374. Misses' Jacket, with Columbian cape, edged with black coney on cape and collar, cape lined with satin, full leg-of-mutton sleeves, buttons to match. Price, all sizes, $7.50.

No. 809. Misses' Jacket. Sizes, 12 to 18 years. Made from fine silk and wool goods. Cut fan back, and trimmed with braid. Price, $9.00.

No. 330. Misses' Double-breasted Jacket, notched collar, umbrella or fan back, Derby effect cape edged with black coney fur. Price, all sizes, 12 to 18 years, $7.50. Colors, black, blue, and tan.

No. 241. Misses' Double-breasted Jacket, umbrella effect cape, entire garment edged with fur. Comes in tan, navy, black, and green. Price, all sizes, $8.50.

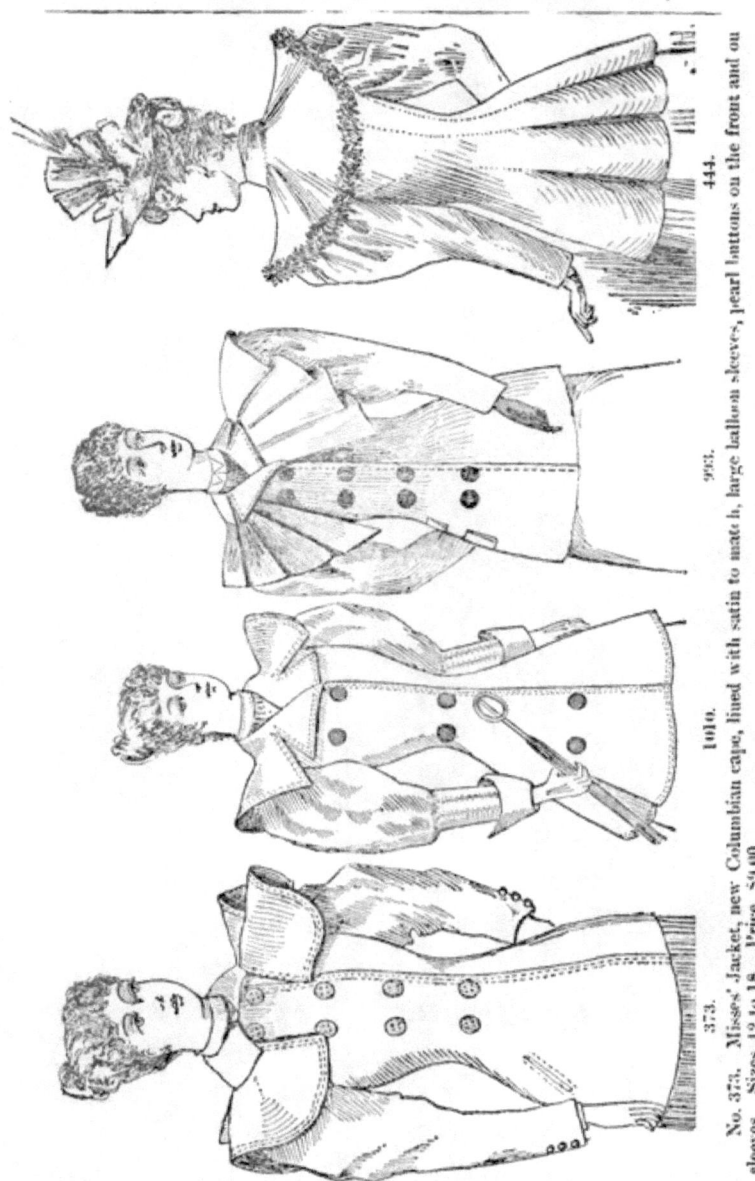

No. 373. Misses' Jacket, new Columbian cape, lined with satin to match, large balloon sleeves, pearl buttons on the front and on sleeves. Sizes, 12 to 18. Price, $9.00.

No. 1010. Misses' Double-breasted Jacket, made in navy and black beaver cloaking, continental collar, large puffed sleeves with cuffs, umbrella back, large buttons. Sizes, 4 to 14 years. Price, $12.00.

No. 993. Misses' Jacket, of gray and blue mixture, also brown mixture, lap pockets, fan back, full butterfly cape, notch collar, horn buttons. Sizes, 12 to 18. Price, $5.00.

No. 444. Cheviot Jacket, 30 inches long, double-breasted, with pearl buttons, Worth cape edged with black coney, umbrella skirt. Colors, black, blue, and green. Handsome, stylish, and warm garment. Price, $9.00.

102.

208.

402.

500.

No. 102. Child's Gretchen, beaver, in blue, black, green, Havana, large butterfly cape, edged with black roney on cape and collar, handsome buttons to match. Price, for 4-year size, $6.50.

No. 208. Gretchen. Sizes, 4 to 14 years. Made from fine plaid and mixed goods, fancy cape, full ruff, and edged with cord to match the cloths. Price, for 4-year size, $6.50. Advance, 25c.

No. 402. Child's Gretchen, butterfly or Derby cape, double-brea-ted, strapped or shirred back. Comes in tan and blue. Price, for 4-year size, $5.00. Advance, 50c. on each size.

No. 500. Child's Gretchen, made with split cape, high shoulders, strap back, with handsome buckle. Comes in desirable assortment of mixed plaids. Price, all sizes, from 4 to 14 years, $5.00.

96.

191.

137.

226.

No. 226. Gretchen. Sizes, 4 to 14 years. Made from fine silk and wool cloths, trimmed with velvet Price, for 4 year size. $9.00. Advance, 50c.

No. 137. Child's double-breasted Gretchen, buttoned to the neck, full gathered skirt, with belt of cloth, umbrella effect cape edged with fur. Price, 4-year size, $5.00. Advance, 50c. on each size.

No. 191. Child's Gretchen, of handsome fancy cloths, latest European cape, trimmed with velvet and heavy cord and tassels to match, full bishop sleeves, buttons to match. Price, for 4-year size, $7.50. Advance, 50c.

No. 96. Child's Gretchen Cloak, umbrella cape, full skirt, extra large sleeves, made in pretty mixtures of brown, tan, and blue. Price, for 4-year size, $5.00. Advance, 25c for each size.

604.   615.   708.

No. 604. Misses' Newmarket. Sizes, 12 to 18 years. Made from fine silk and wool cloth and trimmed with fine gimp. Price, $10.00, all sizes.

No. 615. Misses' Newmarket, with butterfly or Derby cape, double-breasted. Comes in tan or blue. Price, for all sizes, 14 to 18 years, $7.50.

No. 708. Misses' Newmarket, of gray and blue mixtures, fan back, full sleeves, pleated cape, notch collar, horn buttons. Sizes, 12 to 18 years. Price, $8.50.

544.　　　　　515.　　　　　526.

No. 515.　Newmarket, a handsome, stylish garment, cape, lapels, and sleeves entirely new, extreme lengths with full umbrella skirt.　Colors, tan and light brown, diagonals and fancy brown mixtures.　Price, $15.00.

No. 526.　Misses' Newmarket, made in tan, mixtures, or in navy and black cheviots, Columbian collar, large puffed sleeves.　Sizes, 14 to 20 years.　Price, $13.00.

BOSTON, MASS.

690.

965.

962.

610.

No. 690. Neat School Dress of checked, fancy all-wool suiting, with pointed yoke front and back, connected with shoulder epaulettes, soft belt, standing collar, yoke and sleeves trimmed with soutache braid. In blue, green, and brown mixture. Price, for 4-year size, $6.00. Advance, 50c on each size.

No. 965. Child's Dress, made from handsome mixed cloth of silk and wool, velvet front to match goods, edged with pretty cord to match. Price, for 4-year size, $5.00. Advance, 25c.

No. 962. Child's All-wool Dress, made from hop sacking, velvet cuffs, and Bolero Jacket of velvet, belt and rosette of same. Price, for 4-year size, $7.00. Advance, 25c on each size.

No. 610. Very stylish Child's Dress, of all-wool fancy novelty suiting, with full yoke of two-toned bengaline, shirred at neck, plaited silk collar with heading, full leg o' mutton sleeve with shaded silk cuff, full waist front and back, caught at side by steel slide, soft belt, full skirt. Colors, bluish, greenish, and brownish checked mixtures. Price, for 4-year size, $7.00. Advance, 50c on each size.

647.   203.   209.

No. 647. Two-piece Misses' Suit, of all-wool flaked suiting, full skirt trimmed with two rows of heavy corded braid, soft plaited belt, braid trimmed, waist fu'l front and back, gathered shoulder pieces with band of braid near edge, full leg o' mutton sleeve trimmed at wrist with two rows of braid. Colors, bluish and brownish mottled effects. Price, for 14 years, $12.00; 16 years, $13.00.

No. 203. Misses' Two-piece Dress, made from all-wool hop sacking, in all the leading shades, very effective in designs. Price, for 14 years, $15.00. Advance, $1.00 on each size.

No. 209. Misses' Two-piece Dress, made from dark changeable mixtures, waist braided, and fancy silk yoke, as shown. Price, for 14 years, $16.00. Advance, $1.00 on each size.

:

FRENCH CORSETS.

THE "FLEUR DE LIS" CORSET.

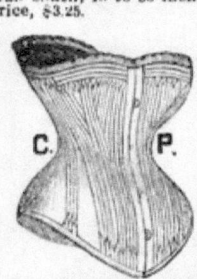

No. 28. Spoon busk, long waist, high bust, white and drab coutil, 18 to 36 inches. Price, $3.25.

No. 263. Sateen, medium length, white and drab. Price, $2.50.

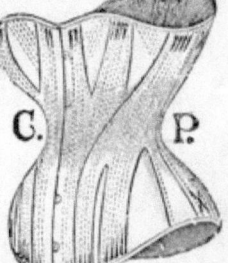

Fine coutil superieur. Perfect shape, 18 to 30 inches. Price, $3.50.

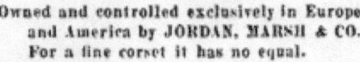

Owned and controlled exclusively in Europe and America by JORDAN, MARSH & CO. For a fine corset it has no equal.

These elegant long-waisted styles hold the first place amongst the corsets of the season, being better adapted than any other to the fashionable attire of the day. The well-known trade-mark, "Fleur de Lis" (with which every genuine pair is stamped), is a guarantee that the materials and workmanship are the best that can be procured.

"FLEUR DE LIS"

Acknowledged to be the best high-priced Corset in America.

We carry them in the following popular styles:—

No 5. Long waist, high bust. Sizes, 18 to 26 inches. Black Italian cloth, fine white coutil and ecru linen. Price, $9.00.

No 5A. Extra long waist, high bust, in fine white coutil, white and ecru linen and black Italian cloth. Sizes, 18 to 30 inches. Price, $11.00.

No. 202. Fine white coutil, medium waist, low bust, for stout figures. Sizes, 19 to 30 inches. Price, $6.00.

No. 302 Medium waist, high bust. Sizes, 18 to 30 inches. In black Italian cloth and fine white coutil. Price, $8.00.

No. 152. The Perfect Shape, white and drab coutil, with sateen stripe, 18 to 30 inches. Price, $2.75.

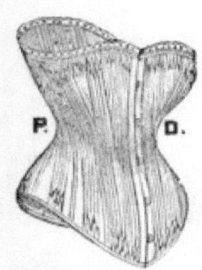

No. 97. Sateen, white and black, very popular, 18 to 30 inches. Price, $3.25.

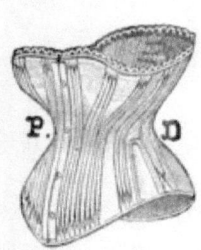

No. 248. Sateen, medium and short lengths. Sizes, 18 to 26. Price, $2.50.

BOSTON, MASS.

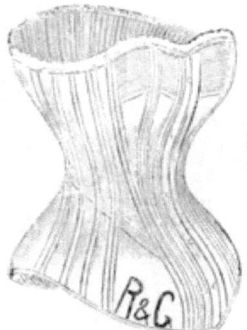

No. 121. Moulded Corset, white and drab jean, medium length, 75c.

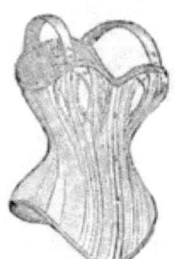

No. 265. Dr. Warner's Health Corset, with tampico bust and shoulder strap, boned with coraline. Price, $1.25.

No. 266. Dr. Warner's Coraline Corset, white and drab, 18 to 30 inches, $1.00; 31 to 36, $1.25.

HER MAJESTY'S CORSET.

We are sole agents for this celebrated Corset, and guarantee every pair we sell. It will wear longer, produce a more magnificent figure, and give more comfort to the wearer than any other.

No. 200. Jean, white, drab, and black, 18 to 30 inches, $2.75. Extra sizes, 25c additional.

No. 250. Jean, sateen straps, white and drab, 18 to 30 inches, $3.25; 31 to 33, $3.50; 34 to 36, $3.75.

No. 295. Black Italian cloth, 18 to 30 inches, $4.00; 31 to 33, $4.50; 34 to 36, $5.00.

No. 400. Black Italian cloth, 18 to 30 inches, $5.00; 31 to 33, $5.50; 34 to 36, $6.00.

No. 172. Imported Sewed Corset, white and drab, $2.

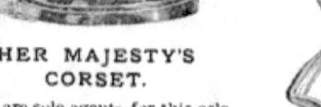

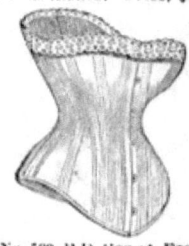

No. 262. Bridal, white only, 18 to 30 inches. Price, $1.

No. 530. P.D. Corset, French coutil, white and drab, $1.75.

No. 267. Thompson patent Nursing Corset, drab, $1.

YOUNG LADIES'.

Style 92. For growing girls, ages 14 to 16 years. Sizes, 18 to 30. Price, $1.00.
Style 42. Young ladies, ages 12 to 14 years. Sizes, 18 to 30. Price, 85c.
Style 32. Misses, ages 10 to 12 years. Sizes, 18 to 30. Price, 75c.
Style 52. Ladies' Double Ve Waist, white and drab imperial jean, $1.00.
Style 62. White and drab sateen. Price, $1.00. Fast black, $1.75.

CORSETS AND WAISTS.

No. 66. Equipoise Waist, stylish, comfortable, hygienic, genuine leather-bone. Pockets allowing the removal of bones without ripping. Prices, white, $2.25; drab, $2.50; black, $3.00.

FERRIS' GOOD SENSE.
Style 204. 50c.

Boys or girls. 4 to 6 years. Superfine material. Buttons up the back. White and drab.

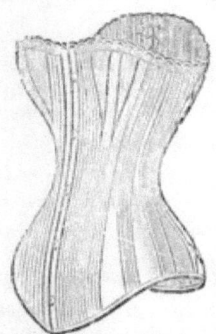

Coronet, Extra long waist, white and drab, 18 to 30 inches. Price, $1.75.

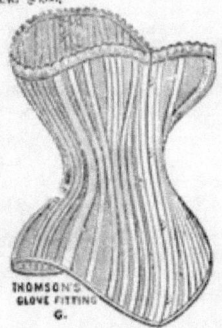

THOMSON'S
GLOVE FITTING
G.

Very long waisted, white and drab, 18 to 30 inches. Price, $1.50. Also Thomson's celebrated R.H. in medium and long waist, white and drab. Sizes 18 to 30 inch, price, $1.00; sizes 31 to 36 inch, $1.25.

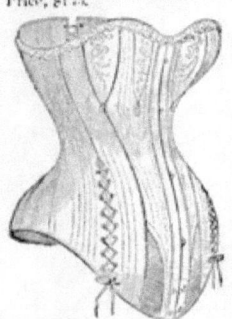

Dr. Warner's Abdominal.
Sizes 18 to 29. Price, $1.50.
"   30 to 36, "   1.75.

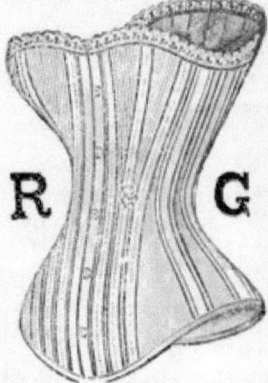

R   G

No. 104. Fast black sateen, extra long waist, $1.75.

FERRIS
GOOD SENSE

Style 264. $1.75.
Black satin jean, fine quality. Fast black; will not crock. Ladies' medium form, long waist. Buttons front, laced back.

Style 219. $1.50.
Ladies' medium form, long waist. Superfine material, extra fine pearl buttons. Cloth-covered pliable steels, front and back. Buttons front, laced back. White and drab.

Style 223. $1.00.
Misses, 12 to 17 years. Superfine material. Bust soft as silk. White and drab.

BOSTON, MASS.

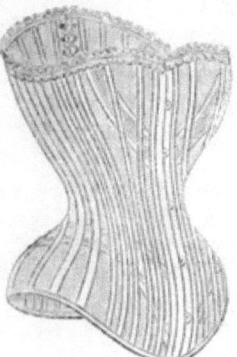

Trophy. This is our great leader, and is, without exception, the best value we have ever been able to offer our patrons at the price. White and drab. 75c.

LADIES' UNION SUITS AND EQUESTRIAN TIGHTS.

These garments are becoming more and more popular every year. There is no garment made that will give the wearer as much comfort and freedom. They are endorsed by the leading physicians of the world. The enormous demand the past season forces us to add many new lines to our stock. Among the most important lines we carry are the Imported Swiss Goods, the Jacksonville and Munsing.

SWISS UNION SUITS.

No. 2G-44. Heavy merino, high neck, long sleeves, ankle length. Colors, white and natural.

Sizes, 2, 3, 4, 5.
Prices, $3.00, 3.25, 3.50, 3.75.

No. 2G-42. Heavy merino, high neck, short sleeves, ankle length. Color, white.

Sizes, 2, 3, 4, 5.
Prices, $3.00, 3.25, 3.50, 3.50.

No. 2G-39. All wool, closed front, low neck, no sleeves, knee length, fancy crochet finish on neck and arm size. Colors, white and black.

Sizes, 2, 3, 4, 5.
Prices, white, $3, 3.25, 3.50, 3 75.
" black, 3.50, 3.50, 4.00, 4.00.

No. 2H-44. All wool, high neck, long sleeves, ankle length, patent shoulder. Color, black.

Sizes, 2, 3, 4, 5.
Prices, $3.50, 3 50, 4.00, 4.00.

No. 2H-42. Black, all wool, short sleeves, ankle length, high neck.

Sizes, 2, 3, 4, 5.
Prices, $3.00, 3.25, 3.50, 3.75.

No. 5B-44. Pure spun silk, high neck, long sleeves, ankle length. Colors, white and black.

Sizes, 3, 4, 5.
Prices, $5.50, 6.00, 6 50.

Same goods, in short sleeves, 50c less on a size.

We carry a large variety of lower grade goods varying in price from $1.00 per suit up.

MUNSING PLAITED SUITS.

No. 221. Winter weight, 80 per cent. wool, long sleeves, high neck, ankle length. Colors, white and natural, price, $2.50; black, $3.00. Sizes, 2, 3, 4, 5.

The same style, short sleeves, in white only. Price, $2.50.

No. 243. All wool, long sleeves, ankle length, high neck. Colors, natural, white, and black. Sizes, 2, 3, 4, 5. Price, $3.00.

No. 245. Extra heavy weight, all wool, high neck, long sleeves, ankle length. Colors, white and natural. Price, $4.00.

JACKSONVILLE.

No. 500. Merino, light weight, high neck, long sleeves, ankle length. Colors, natural and white.

Sizes, 2, 3, 4, 5.
Prices, $3.50, 3.75, 4.00, 4.25.

No. 800-10. Extra heavy silk, high neck, ankle length, long sleeves. Flesh color. Sizes, 3, 4, 5. Price for either size, $15.00.

EQUESTRIAN TIGHTS.

No. 426. Black all-wool medium weight Tights, in both open and closed, knee length.

Sizes, 2, 3, 4, 5.
Prices, $2.50, 2.50, 2.50, 2.50.

Same quality, ankle length. Price, $2.75.

Heavy weight, all wool, black, ankle length, all sizes. Price, $3.00.

Pure silk, winter weight, knee length, all sizes. Price, $6.50.

BOSTON, MASS.

COLORED SKIRTS AND KNIT GOODS.

No. 1100. Gray Melton, with box pleat and piped band above. Price, 5c.

No. 1000. Gray Melton, box pleat trimmed with braid, piped band above. Price, $1.00.

No. 1053. Best Melton, deep shirred, embroidered ruffle, band above. Price, $1.75.

 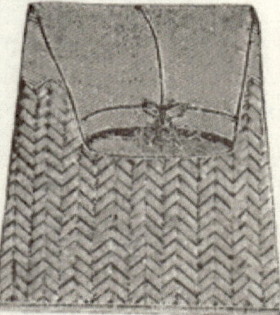 

No. 1850. Fast Black Lasting, deep box pleat, band above. Price, $1.25, 1.50, 1.75.

We also carry in stock at all times the best quality English Moreen Skirts in grays and black. Price, $2.25.

No. 1201. Black Quilted Lasting Skirt, velvet bound, fast color. Price, $1.00; better quality, $1.25, 1.50 1.75, 2, 2.50, 3.

Silk Skirts in a large variety of styles, in both colors and black. Price, $5.00 to 15.00.

No. 1728. Fast Black Lasting, shirred ruffle. Price, $1.25, 1.50, 1.75, 2.00, 2.50.

Ladies' and children's black worsted Leggins.

No. 200.	Size,	2,	3,	4,	5,	6,	7,	8.
	Length,	17,	19,	21,	24,	27,	30,	33 in.
	Price,	37,	40,	45,	50,	55,	55,	62c.
No. 300.	"		50,	55,	60,	70,	80,	90c, $1 00.
No. 800.	"		62,	70,	75,	85,	95c,	$1.10, 1.25.

No. 134   Ladies' hand-crocheted Hood, large size, with long tab ends, trimmed with fine quality ribbon bows, $1.50; same style, lighter weight, $1 25.

Ladies' Shoulder or Breakfast Shawls in various styles and sizes, hand-made, vary in price from $1 00 to $2.25.

No. 124.   Ladies' Shoulder Cape, hand-made, medium weight, $1 25.

Ladies' Cardigan Jackets with sleeves, in plain colors, medium size, $1.75; extra size, $2.00. Better quality medium size, $2.25; extra size, $2.75.

No. 185.   Beaded Fascinator, with tab ends, very handsome   Price, $1.25.

No. 188.   Beaded Fascinator, not quite as elaborate as 185   Price, 75c

Children's Hoods in a large variety of styles, vary in price from 50c to $1 25.

Ladies' Knit Underskirts, in short, medium, and long lengths, in several styles of plain and fancy stitch.   Popular colors.   Prices varying from 98c to $3.50

Ladies' Fascinators in a large variety of styles and sizes, hand-made, 25c to $1.50.

No. 267.   Mexican Jacket in plain colors and stripes, medium size, 75c; extra size, $1.00.

No. 260.   Cardigan Jacket in plain colors and stripes, medium size, $1.00; extra size, in plain colors only, $1.50.   Same style, better quality, medium size, $1.75; extra size, $2.00.

FRENCH UNDERWEAR.

Owing to the enormous demand for French Underwear, we have been forced to increase our department from season to season, until at the present time we have one of the largest departments in the United States. Our buyer visits the leading European manufacturers every season, enabling us at all times to display the latest and newest creations in this class of merchandise.

Corset Covers, hand embroidered, vary in price from 75c to $2.50.

Corset Covers trimmed with lace, fine embroidery, and ribbons, vary in price from $2.75 to $6.50.

Chemises, hand embroidered, vary in price from 69c to $5.

Chemises, trimmed with lace, ribbons, and embroidery, vary in price from $1.50 to $10.

Drawers, hand embroidered, range in price from $1 to $3.50.

Drawers, trimmed with laces, ribbons, and embroidery, vary in price from $2 to $15.

Night Robes, hand embroidered, vary in price from $1 to $6.

Night Robes, trimmed with laces, ribbon, and embroidery, vary in price from $3 to $30.

Skirts, hand embroidered, vary in price from $1.25 to $4.50.

Skirts, trimmed with lace and embroidery, vary in price from $5 to $30.

We also carry in connection with above, a superb assortment of Silk Negligée Gowns, Skirts, Drawers, and Chemises.

LADIES' AND CHILDREN'S APRONS.

No. 1008.　Ladies' Apron of fine striped muslin.　Price, 25c.
No. 600.　Child's Lawn Apron.　Collar and sleeves edged with fine lace.　Price, 75c.
No. 503　Child's Lawn Apron.　Embroidered ruffle on neck and sleeves.　Price, 80c.
No. 504.　Child's Lawn Apron.　Ruffles and yoke trimmed with embroidered edge.　Price, $1.25.
No. 967.　Nurse Apron.　Fine lawn, 9-inch hem.　Price, 25c.
No. 612.　Child's Apron.　Ruffles and sleeves of embroidered Persian trimming, edged with lace.　Price, $1.50

LADIES' NIGHT ROBES.

407. Muslin, tucked yoke, edged with Hamburg. Price, 50c.

216. Fine cotton, yoke of insertions and tucks, cam. ruffle. 75c.

487. Muslin, Hamburg insertion and edging. Price, 75c.

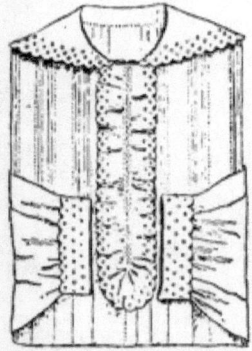

477. Muslin, solid yoke of Hamburg insertion and edging. $1.00.

600. Cotton, tucked yoke, collar, cuffs, and front of yoke of fine embroidery. Price, $1.25.

517. Muslin, Hamburg insertion and edging. Price, $1.00.

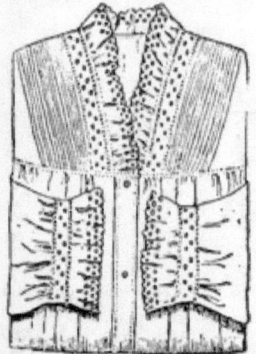

100. Home-made garment of fine heavy cotton, plain collar and cuffs, either Hubbard or sack. Price, $1.00.

650. Fine cotton, yoke of tucks, insertion, and edging. $1.50.

110. Long cam., yoke Val. lace, inser'ns, double ruffle on neck. $1.10.

LADIES' CHEMISES AND DRAWERS.

No. 306. Muslin, fine embroidered ruffle, with twelve fine tucks above. Price, 75c.

No. 307. Cambric, Platte lace insertion and edging. Price, 85c.

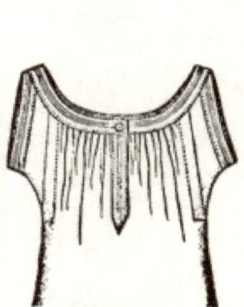

C. Corded band, heavy cotton, 50c. Same style, cheaper cotton, 39c.

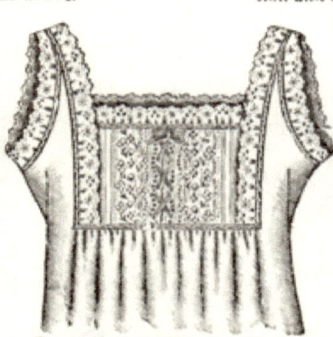

E. Pride of the West muslin, embroidered yoke and edging, with ribbon run through. Price, 75c.

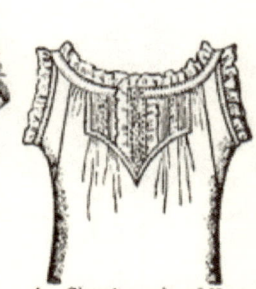

A. Chemise, yoke of Hamburg insertions and tucks, finished with cambric ruffle. 50c.

No. 300. Made of fine quality cotton, Hamburg ruffle and tucks. Price, 50c.

No. 302. Muslin Drawers, with tucked cambric ruffle, and tucks above. Price, 50c.

Boys' Night Shirts, heavy cotton, collar, cuffs, and pocket trimmed with feather-edge braid. Sizes, 5 to 9 years, 75c.

Children's cotton flannel Night Drawers, 2 to 8 years, 49c.

No. 469. Misses' Lonsdale cambric Corset Cover. Sizes, 30 to 32. Price, 25c.

We carry in stock at all times a full and complete assortment of Chemises and Drawers, ranging in price from 25c to $5.00 each.

BOSTON, MASS.

CORSET COVERS AND COMBINATIONS.

No. 600. Skirt and Corset Cover trimmed with emb. Price, 75c.

No. 507. Cambric torchon lace, with ribbon run through. Price, 75c.

No. 620. Corset Cover and Skirt combined, cambric, trimmed with fine emb. Price, $1.00.

No. 143. Corset Cover, heavy cotton, tucked front, neck trimmed with Hamburg. Price, 25c.

No. 451. Cambric, fine embroidery. Price, 50c.

No. 181. Cambric, fine embroidery. Price, 50c.

No. 562. Cambric, Hamburg insertion and edging. Price, 50c.

Jersey Corset Cover. Price, 25, 50, 75c., and $1.00.

No. 508. Fine durable cotton, insertions and edge of neat Hamburg. Price, 37½c.

No. 214. Walking Skirt, Lonsdale ruffle, trimmed with Valenciennes lace and insertion between tucks. Price, $2.

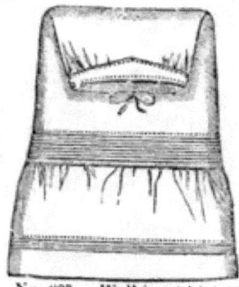

No. 207. Walking Skirt of fine, durable cotton, with a deep tucked cambric ruffle and tucks above. Price, $1.00.

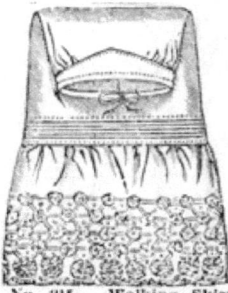

No. 215. Walking Skirt, with a deep ruffle of exquisite embroidery. Price, $3.00.

No. 210. Walking Skirt, with ruffle of linen tor. lace insert'n and edge between tucks, and tucks above. Price, $1.50.

No. 2. Ladies' Bell-shaped Walking Skirt, deep flounces of fine emb. Price, $6.00.

Same style, 1 ruffle. Price, $4.00.

No. 205.

No. 209. Walking Skirt, with deep tuck'd ruffle, trimmed with torchon lace. Price, $1.00.

No. 205. Bell-shaped Skirt, deep flounces of choice embroidery, $5. 1 ruffle, $4 00.

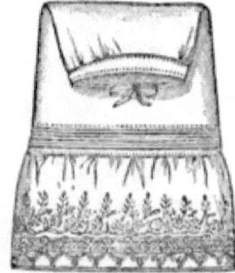

No. 208. Walking Skirt, with a deep Hamburg ruffle, in variety of neat patterns. $1.00.

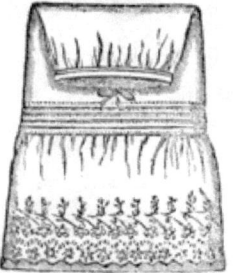

No. 200. Walking Skirt, fine Hamburg ruffle. Price, 75c.

No. 206. Walking Skirt, with a tucked ruffle, trimmed with Platte Val. lace. Price, $1.50.

BOSTON, MASS.

INFANTS' WARDROBES.

No. 20. Infants' Wardrobe, consisting of 20 pieces, for $12.00. This outfit is very popular.

2 Flannel Bands, 25c	$0.50
2 " Pinning Blankets, 50c	1.00
2 Flannel Skirts, $1.00	2.00
2 Saxony Shirts, 37½c	.75
4 Cambric Night Slips, 25c	1.00
1 " Day Dress	1.25
1 " " "	1.00
2 " " Dresses, 50c	1.00
1 Baptismal Robe	2.00
1 Flannel Shoulder Shawl	1.00
2 pair hand-crocheted Bootees, 25c	.50
	$12.00

No. 12. Infants' Wardrobe, consisting of 15 pieces, for $10.00.

2 Knit Saxony Bands, 37½c	$0.75
2 " " Shirts, 37½c	.75
2 Flannel Pinning Blankets, 75c	1.50
2 Flannel Skirts, $1.25	2.50
2 Cambric Night Slips, 37½c	.75
2 " Day " 50c	1.00
1 Baptismal Robe	2.25
2 pair hand-crocheted Socks, 25c	.50
	$10.00

No. 171. Infants' Wardrobe, consisting of 18 pieces, for $15.00.

2 pair hand-made crocheted Bootees.
2 Saxony Shirts.
2 Knit Bands.
2 Flannel Pinning Blankets.
2 " Skirts.
1 Embroidered Shawl.
4 Cambric Slips.
2 Handsome Dresses.
1 Basket (Pink or Blue).
This wardrobe is very cheap and exceedingly popular.

No. 17. The above cut is an illustration of our great leader in Infants' Wardrobes, consisting of 17 pieces, for $5.50.

2 All-wool Shirts.
2 Flannel Bands.
2 pair hand-crocheted Bootees.
2 Pinning Blankets.
2 Flannel Skirts.
1 Shoulder Shawl.
4 Slips.
1 Day Dress.
1 Trimmed Dress.

No 18. Infants' Wardrobe, containing 23 pieces, for $18.00.

1 Baptismal Robe.
7 Handsome Dresses, assorted styles.
2 Cambric Night Slips.
2 Flannel Skirts.
2 " Pinning Blankets.
1 Embroidered Flannel Blanket.
2 Knit Bands.
2 Shirts.
2 pair hand-crocheted Bootees.
2 Quilted Bibs.
This entire outfit only $18.00.

No. 50. Infants' entire outfit, containing 41 pieces, $50.00.

6 Linen Shirts.
2 Fine Cashmere Shirts.
2 " " Bands.
2 Flannel Pinning Blankets.
2 Plain Flannel Skirts.
1 Embroidered Flannel Skirt.
4 Trimmed Cambric Skirt.
4 " " Night Slips.
1 Embroidered Flannel Wrapper.
1 Embroidered Flan. Blanket.
6 Cambric Dresses, handsomely trimmed, assorted styles.
1 Handsome Baptismal Robe.
1 Baptismal Lace Cap.
4 Embroidered Quilted Bibs.
1 " Flannel Sacque.
2 pair Crocheted Socks.
2 pieces Linen Diaper.
2 " Cotton "
This beautiful outfit only $50.00.

INFANTS' WEAR.

No. 5. Infants' Knit Boots, in cream white. Price, 50c.

No. 501. Infants' all-wool flannel Skirt. Deep hem. Price, $1.00.
No. 1. Infants' all-wool embroidered flannel Skirt. Price, $1.75.
No. 596. Infants' fine quality flannel Skirt. Seams and hem feather stitched in silk. Price, $1.50.
No. 931. Infants' fine cambric Skirt. Price, 65c.
No. 229. Infants' French cambric Skirt, trimmed with dainty embroidery, featherstitched above. Price, $1.25.
No. 926. Infants' fine Lonsdale cambric Skirt, trimmed with dainty embroidery, 3 clusters tucks above. Price, $1.00.

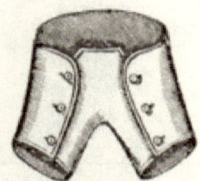

No. 7. Infants' Canneld Diaper. Price, 65c.

INFANTS' AND CHILDREN'S DRESSES.

No. 479. Infants' Night Slip, fine cambric, trimmed with dainty embroidery. Price, 69c.

The above cut represents our great leader. No. 1 is an Infants' long Dress, yoke of feather stitching and fagoting; No. 2, Child's Dress, ages 6 mos. to 3 yrs., yoke of insertion and fagoting. Skirts of both have a deep hem with fagoting above. Price of either, 98c.

No. 1420. Infants' long Dress, yoke of fine embroidery skirt with deep hem, fagoting above. Price, $1.50.

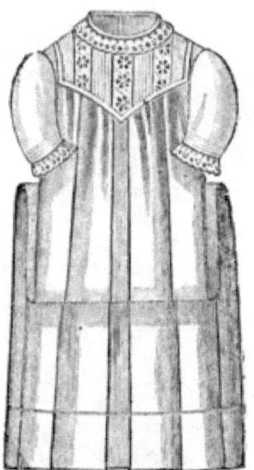

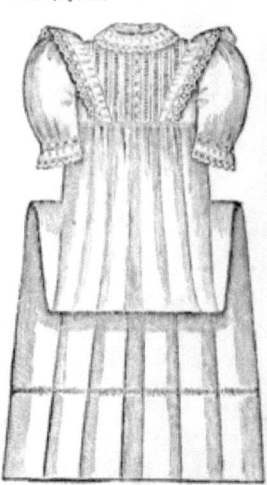

No. 432. Infants' long Dress of French cambric, dainty yoke of embroidery and tucks. Price, 98c.

No. 401. Infants' long Dress, yoke of dainty embroidery and tucks. Price, 75c.

No. 1431. Infants' long Dress dainty yoke of embroidery and tucks, deep hem. Price, $1.75.

CHILDREN'S SHORT DRESSES.

No. 1219. Child's cambric Dress, yoke of tucks finished with feather-edge braid. 6 mos. to 2 years. Price, 75c.

No 1298. Dress of French cambric, shirred at neck and sleeves, ruffle over shoulders, neck and sleeves edged with lace. 6 mos. to 3 years. Price, 75c.

No. 101. Dress of French cambric, yoke of fine tucks, puffs over shoulders, neck and sleeves trim'd with dainty embroidery. 6 mos. to 3 years. Price, $1.25.

No. 1162. Dress of fine nainsook, handsomely trimmed with delicate embroidery. 1 to 3 yrs. Price, $2.50.

No. 1277. Dress of French nainsook, yoke of rich embroidery, skirt trimmed to match. 1 to 3 years. Price, $2.75.

No. 1062. Dress of embroidered muslin, yoke of embroidery, with puffs over shoulders. 1 to 3 yrs. Price, $2.00.

JORDAN, MARSH AND COMPANY,

LONG AND SHORT COATS.

No. 12 Infants' embroidered cashmere Cloak. $2.50.

No. 10. Infants' Cloak, embroidered. Price, $2.00.

No. 14. Infants' Cloak, embroidered. Price, $2.75.

No. 126. Fancy wool, velvet & braid trim'g. 2, 3, 4 yrs. $4.75.

No. 763. Cloak, eiderdown, edged with a silk cord. $3.75.

No. 120. Plaid, full sleeves, braid trim'g. 2, 3, 4 yrs. $2.50.

No. 174. Eiderdown, trim'd with angora fur. 1, 2, 3 yrs. Price, $2.89.

No. 130. Fancy wool material, trimmed with worsted braid. 2, 3, 4 yrs. $3.50.

No. 149. Fine plain all-wool material, trim'd with velvet and braid. 2, 3, 4 yrs. $8.50.

BOSTON, MASS.

CHILDREN'S CAPS.

No. 1032. Embroidered surah silk, white only. 79c.

No. 1211. Silk bengaline, trimmed with velvet and animal head. Popular colors. Price, $3.

No. 1309. Bengaline, trimmed with black fur. Popular colors. Price, $2.50.

No. 1234. Bengaline trim. with velvet. Popular colors. Price, $2.25.

No. 1000. Bengaline, in cream white only. Price, 79c.

No. 1041. Bengaline, cream white only. Price, $1.

No. 1236. Bonnet of bengaline. Popular colors. $1.75.

No. 1037. Embr. surah silk Cap, white. $1.50.

No. 1233. Bengaline, high crown, trim. with velvet. $2.50.

No. 1340. Bengaline, trim. with plush fur. $2.

No. 1025. Embr. surah silk Cap, in white. $1.25.

GENERAL REMARKS.

We have a complete line of Novelties for boys of all ages, and are also prepared to make to order anything that customers might desire.

We have every facility for the manufacture of the finest custom work, and are also prepared to suggest to customers the correct thing for every occasion.

By writing to us, stating what the garment is wanted for, we will send the correct article.

White Suits, in velvet, serge, and flannel, for weddings, a specialty.

We are complete Outfitters, and are prepared to show everything suitable for boys' wear.

DIRECTIONS FOR MEASUREMENTS.

Name........................ ....Age......................

COAT.

Length of Sleeve, 1 to 2, and 3.............................

Around Breast, under arm, over vest, 4...................

Full length of Coat in back..............................

SHORT PANTS.

Waist, 5...

Outside length of Pants, 5 to 6 ....

Inside seam...

Around bottom at knee............. ....

LONG PANTS.

Inside seam to 7........ ....

DESCRIPTION OF FORM.

MEASURES TO BE TAKEN UNDER JACKET, EXCEPT FOR OUTSIDE GARMENTS.

BOSTON, MASS.

ZOUAVE KILT. JACKET KILT. REEFER SUIT. NORFOLK SUIT.

"Zouave" Kilt. Sizes, 2½ to 6 years. Plain blue and mixed cloths. Prices, $3.50, 4, 5, 6, 8, 10. Same in blue and black velvet. Prices, $5.50, 7, 8, 10, 12. Lawn blouses to be worn with these suits. Prices, 50c, 75, $1, to 3.50.

"Jacket" Kilt. Sizes, 2½ to 6 years. Plain colors and fancy mixtures, with plaid or mixed blouse or vest front. Prices, $3.75, 5, 6, 7, 8.

"Reefer" Suit. Sizes, 4 to 8 years. In plain and mixed cloths trimmed with braid, with or without gilt buttons. Prices, $3.50, 4, 5, 6, 8.

"Norfolk" Suit. Sizes, 4 to 10 years. Handsome mixed cloths, also plain colors. Prices, $5, 6, 8.

Send for samples of our "Hub Combination" Suit, extra pants, overcoat, and cap. Price, $10.

ZOUAVE.   ENSIGN.   JERSEY SUIT.   RUSSIAN.

"Square Zouave" Suit. Sizes, 4 to 8 years. This is the leading novelty for small boys. They are made in mixed goods, Scotch effects, plaids, and stripes. Prices, $3.50, 4, 5, 6, 8, 10. In blue and black velvet, trimmed with silk braid. Prices, $5, 6, 7, 8, 9, 10, 12. In blue tricot, French and German crepe, also diagonals. Prices, $5, 6, 7, 8, 10, 12.

"Ensign" Suit. Sizes, 4 to 8 years. New styles this season. Plain and fancy mixtures. Prices, $5, 6, 7, 8.

"Jersey" Suit. Sizes, 4 to 10 years. In navy blue, plain, and trimmed with silk braid. Prices, $3.50, 4, 5, 6.

"Russian" Suit. This suit is particularly adapted for boys from 4 to 8 years. It is the newest thing we are showing this season, and we anticipate that it will meet the demand for something new and nobby for the little fellows. It is made in plain blue and fancy mixtures. Prices, according to quality, $5, 6, 7, 8, 10, 12.

Send for samples of our "Tug of War" Suit. Sizes, 6 to 15 years. Re-enforced seat and knee, tapped seams. Price, $5.

BOSTON, MASS.

LENOX.   LAKEWOOD.   BEACON.

"Lenox." Sizes, 4 to 16 years. Single-breasted suits of Scotch mixtures, plaids, and stripes. Prices, $3.50, 4, 5, 6, 7, 8, 10. Same in black cheviot, always in stock to fill mourning orders. Prices, $6, 8, 10, 12.

"Lakewood." Sizes, 4 to 8 years. Plain and fancy mixtures, with or without braid, also small collar instead of sailor collars, if desired. Prices, plain, $3.50, 4, 5; trimmed, $5, 6, 8.

"Beacon." Sizes, 6 to 16 years. The fashionable double-breasted suit, in imported Scotch mixtures and fancy worsteds, plaids, and plain. Prices, $7.50, 8, 10, 12, 14. Same in domestic cloths, plain colors and fancy mixtures. Prices, $3.50, 4, 5, 6, 8, 10.

"Harvard" Suit. Sizes, 10 to 16 years. Three-button cutaway with vest, in Scotch mixtures, cheviots, and fancy worsteds and cassimeres. Prices, $5, 6, 8, 10, 12. Same in blue and black diagonal and blue tricots, for dress. Prices, $7, 8, 10, 12, 14, 16. This suit is also made in black cheviot, blue and black diagonals, and fancy worsteds, for dress wear. We have them bound with silk braid and plain stitched edges. Prices, $5, 6, 7, 8, 9, 10, 12.

Our "Hub Combination" Suit. Extra pants, overcoat, and cap, all complete, $10. Send for samples.

A Whole Winter's Outfit for $10.00.

Our Great Leader, the
HUB
COMBINATION SUIT,

With Overcoat, Hat, and Extra Pair of
Pants, all to match, for

$10.00.

SIZES, 6 TO 15 YEARS.

These suits are cut in the new three-button, double-breasted jacket, and are trimmed in the best manner. The overcoats are cut with a long detachable cape with large collar, and can be worn either as an ulster or cape overcoat. These have handsome plaid linings.

The hats are all made in the popular English turban shape.

These combinations are made in short pants ONLY, and have been sold by us for a number of years with great success, and we can safely recommend them to our customers.

SAMPLES SENT.

Mail Orders Will Receive Careful Attention.

$5.00 PER SUIT. $5.00 PER SUIT.

"TUG OF WAR,"
4 TO 15 YEARS.

Knowing the demand for an irresistible wearing quality Child's Suit at a low price, we have decided to fill this want, and take pleasure in calling your attention to our "Tug of War" suits, which are manufactured in sizes 4 to 15 years, and sold by us at the nominal price of $5.00 per suit. They are cut double-breasted, and have re-enforced seat and knees, and taped seams, making a wear-resisting suit.

We guarantee these goods to be strictly all-wool, and the best wearing material of any goods offered at this price.

Samples sent upon application.

Extra pants to these suits, if desired, at $1.50.

BOSTON, MASS.

| Single-breasted. | Double-breasted. | Double-breasted. | Chesterfield. |

"Single-breasted Sack" Suit. Ages, 14 to 18 years. This suit is cut single-breasted, and is made in same materials as the double-breasted suit. Prices, $7.50, 8, 9, 10, 12 to 18.

Same in blue and black diagonals for dress suits. Prices, $16, 18, 20, 22.

"Double-breasted Sack" Suit. Ages, 14 to 18 years. This is the fashionable double-breasted sack suit. We have them in broken checks, cassimeres, plain cheviots, plaids, and stripes, all the new shades of this season's productions. Prices, $8, 10, 12 to 20.

"Tuxedo" Dress Suits. For youths, 16 to 19 years. Made of black diagonal, the coat lined throughout or only faced with black silk. Prices, $18, 20, 22, 24.

"D. B. Coat." Sizes, 14 to 19 years. The fashionable double-breasted top coat, in fancy frieze and blue and black kerseys and beavers. Prices, $10, 12, 14 to 20.

"Chesterfield." Sizes, 14 to 19 years. Single-breasted sack overcoat, made in plain and fancy materials, suitable for dress overcoat for fall and winter. Prices, $8, 10, 12, 14, 16, 18.

A full line of odd long pants always in stock. Prices, $2, 2.50, 3, 3.50, 4, 5, 6.

BOSTON, MASS.

REEFER.   TRIPLE CAPE.   CAPE COAT.   ULSTER.

"Reefers." Sizes, 4 to 8 years. In plain blue, with sailor collar and gilt buttons. Prices, $4, 5, 6 to 10. Same style, in fancy mixtures. Prices, $4.50, 5, 6, 7, 8, 9, 10.

"Triple Cape." Sizes, 3 to 6 years. The newest coat this season, made with three capes of stylish mixtures and plain colors. Prices, according to quality, $5, 6, 7, 8, 10, 12.

"Kilt Overcoat." Sizes, 3 to 7 years. In fancy plaids and stripes, also plain colors. These coats are cut double-breasted and extra long. Prices, $3.50, 4, 5, 6, 7, 8, 10.

"Hood Ulster." Sizes, 4 to 10 years. This is the newest and most desirable garment this season for boys of the above age. They are made in fancy mixtures, have wide belt, and the hoods are lined with silk to match the goods. Prices, according to quality, $6, 8, 9, 10, 12, 14.

Plain Ulsters without hood or belt in same sizes and goods. $5, 6, 7, 8, 10.

We have the best line of Odd Pants, 4 to 15 years, ever shown, and at the lowest prices. 50, 75c., $1, 1.50, 2.

BOSTON, MASS.

| APE OVERCOAT. | BOYS' REEFER. | CAPE ULSTER. | STORM ULSTER. |

"Cape Overcoats." Sizes, 7 to 13 years. In plaids, stripes, mixtures, and plain colors. Prices, $5, 6, 7, 8, 10, 12.

"Reefer." Sizes, 4 to 16 years. In blue and brown chinchillas, blue beaver, Irish frieze, and Scotch mixtures, with or without velvet collars and plaid or plain linings. Prices, according to quality, $5, 6, 7, 8, 9, 10, 12, 14.

"Cape Ulsters." Sizes, 10 to 14 years. These coats are made with long detachable capes, large collar, and can be worn either as ulster or cape overcoat. Prices, $7.50, 8, 9, 10, 12, 14, 16.

"Storm Ulsters." Sizes, 10 to 19 years. For young men, in handsome frieze, also smooth goods. We have several styles of cloths in these coats. Prices, $7, 8, 9, 10, 12 to 20.

All our Cape Overcoats and Ulsters are made two to four inches longer than ordinary ready-made coats.

Our $5 Reefer for boys 4 to 16 years is the best ever shown for the money.

BOSTON, MASS.

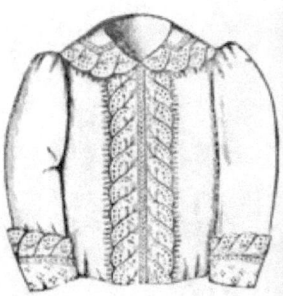

LAWN BLOUSE.

THE STAR SHIRT WAIST.

FLANNEL BLOUSE.

"Star" Shirt Waist. Sizes, 4 to 12 years. Includes an exhaustless variety of patterns in percales, linens, and cambrics. Prices, 75c, $1, 1 25, 1.50. Other makes and styles, unlaundered. Prices, 25, 50c. White waists, linen collars and cuffs. Prices, $1, 1.25, 1.50. White waists, all linen. Price, $1.50.

Lawn Blouse. Sizes, 3 to 6 years. Plain ruffled collar, cuffs, and down front. Prices, 50, 75c, $1. Lawn Blouse, Hamburg trimmed. Prices, $1, 1.50, 2, up.

Flannel Blouse. Sizes, 6 to 14 years. Gray, blue, and brown. Prices, $1, 1.50, 2.

CUSTOM TAILORING DEPARTMENT FOR MEN, YOUTHS, AND BOYS.

We will gladly send samples and prices to any address. All garments made from self-measurement can only be executed at the customer's risk. Every care will, however, be taken to produce a satisfactory fit. We have a fine line of woollens to select from, being extensive importers and dealers in Foreign and Domestic Fabrics. We will give special attention in filling all orders in this department. All work guaranteed. Clerical work and liveries a specialty.

NECESSARY MEASUREMENTS FOR OUTFITS.

Plain Clothes. Directions for Measurement. To be taken in inches.

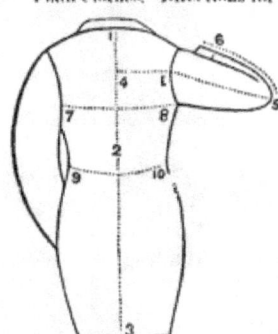

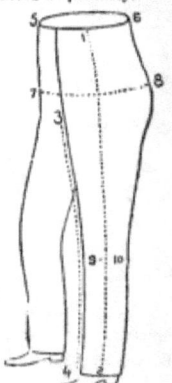

Full height............feet............

1 to 2, length of waist from bottom of collar to hip button. 1 to 3, entire length of coat. 4 to 5, from seam in centre of back to elbow. 5 to 6, from elbow to wrist. 7 to 8, circumference of chest, over the waistcoat. 9 to 10, circumference of waist, over the waistcoat. Style of coat. What pockets. Edges, bound or stitched.

From O at centre of back of the neck round the inside edge of the collar, to height required for top button at P. Continue from top button to R for length in front. Round the breast and round the waist. With or without collar. Double or single breasted.

1 to 2, full length of trousers. 3 to 4, inside leg. 5 to 6, round waist. 7 to 8, round hips. 9 to 10, round knee. Cross or side pockets.

A Word to our Patrons.

By reason of our Mail Order Department we are virtually next door to you. There is nothing in our vast establishment that you cannot have precisely as if you stood before our counters, and at the same price. You can save time, money, and the annoyances attending shopping in person, by ordering what you desire through our Mail Order Department. Our Mail Order Clerks will stand in your stead, and exercise their trained taste. They are here for that purpose. We educate them for this especial work.

How to Order by Mail.

In ordering please state the amount of money you enclose. Write plainly your name, town, and State. Always mention *how* goods are to be sent, whether by mail or express. If by mail, always enclose a sufficient amount to cover the postage, which must be prepaid. If there is a surplus left, it will be returned to you by mail in a separate envelope, with an itemized bill. Postage rates are one cent an ounce, but the parcel must not weigh over four pounds, as that is the limit. Express charges can be paid when goods are delivered. Goods will be sent by express C.O.D. when desired, but cannot be sent in that way by mail. We are not responsible for unregistered letters containing money, or merchandise packages. Registry fee is eight cents additional to postage. The safest way to remit is by money orders or registered mail.

Samples of Dress Goods, Woollens, Silks, Satins, and Velvets, sent free upon request.

Respectfully,

JORDAN, MARSH & CO.,

BOSTON, MASS.

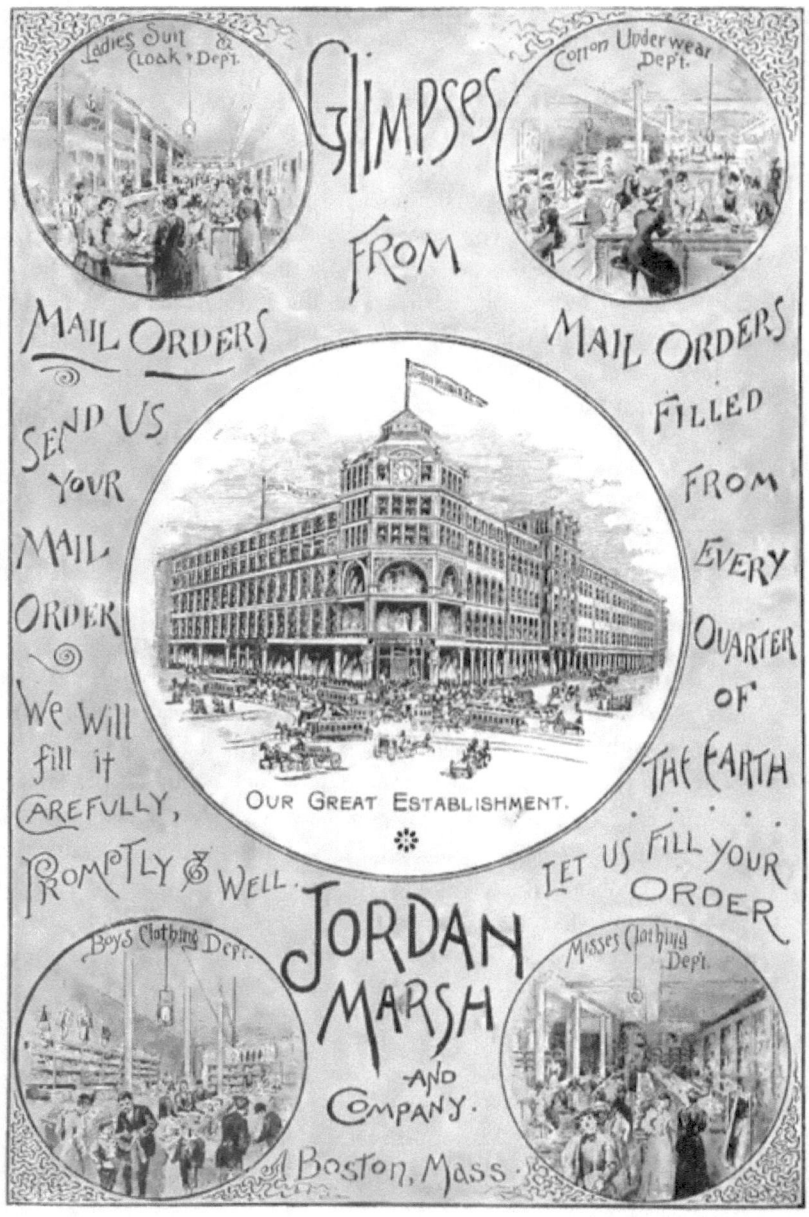

GLIMPSES FROM

MAIL ORDERS

SEND US YOUR MAIL ORDER

We will fill it CAREFULLY, PROMPTLY & WELL.

OUR GREAT ESTABLISHMENT.

MAIL ORDERS FILLED FROM EVERY QUARTER OF THE EARTH

LET US FILL YOUR ORDER

JORDAN MARSH AND COMPANY.

Boston, Mass.